To Cher and Trixie,
who are first in my book

This book is set in Century 725/Monotype; Grilled Cheese BTN/Fontbros; Billy/Fontspring

Printed in Malaysia
Reinforced binding

First Edition, September 2010
30 29 28 27 26 25 24 23 22 21 20
FAC-029191-19207
ISBN: 978-1-4231-3308-7

Library of Congress Cataloging-in-Publication Data on file.

Visit www.hyperionbooksforchildren.com and www.pigeonpresents.com

An ELEPHANT & PIGGIE Book

Hyperion Books for Children / New York
AN IMPRINT OF DISNEY BOOK GROUP

8

13

The reader is reading these word bubbles!

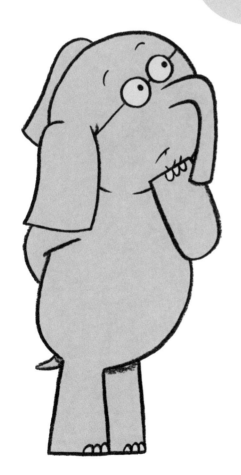

THAT IS

SO COOL!

24

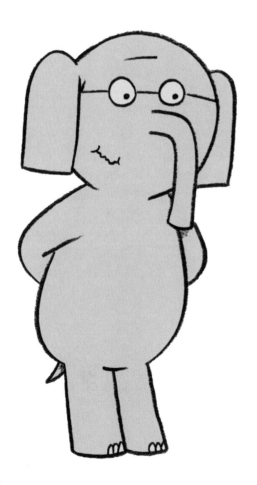

Ha!

Ha!

Ha!

Ha!

Ha!

Hee!
Ha!
Hee!
Ha!
Ha!
Ha!
Hee!
Ha!
Ha!
Ha!
Hee!
Hee!
Ha!
Ha!
Hee!
Hee!
Ha!
Hee!
Hee!
Ha!
Hee!
Ha!
Hee!
Hee!
Hee!
Ha!

Hee!
Ha!
Ha!
Hee!
Hee!
Ha!
Hee!
Ha!
Hee!
Hee!
Ha!
Ha!
Hee!
Hee!
Ha!
Ha!
Hee!
Ha!
Hee!
Ha!
Ha!

Page 57.

49

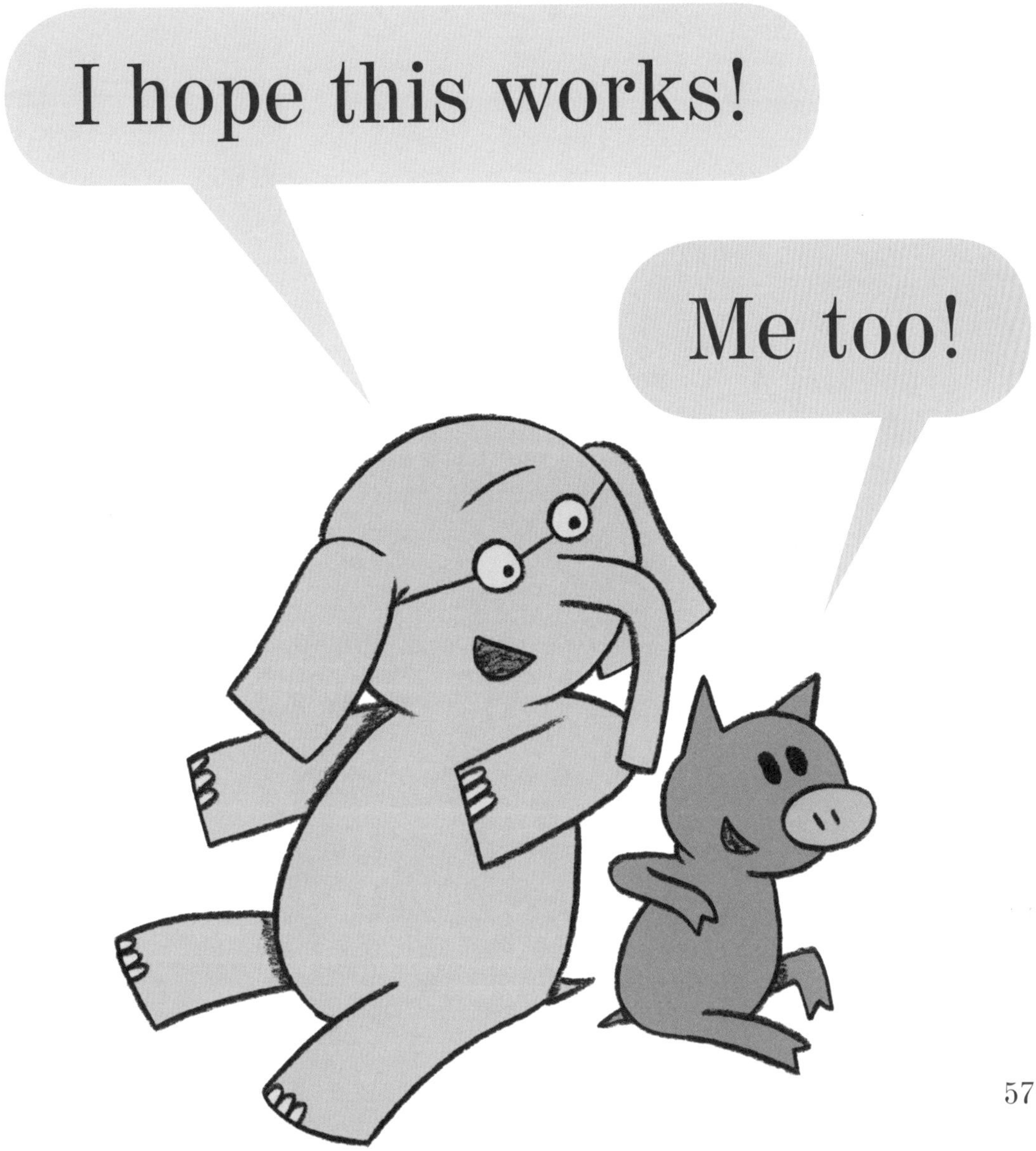
I hope this works!
Me too!

Have you read all of Elephant and Piggie's funny adventures?